Pig in

READZⓄNE

ReadZone Books Limited

50 Godfrey Avenue
Twickenham
TW2 7PF
UK

First published in this edition 2014

© in this edition ReadZone Books Limited 2014
© in text Vivian French 2005
© in illustrations Tim Archbold 2005

Vivian French has asserted her right under the Copyright Designs
and Patents Act 1988 to be identified as the author of this work.

Tim Archbold has asserted his right under the Copyright Designs
and Patents Act 1988 to be identified as the illustrator of this work.

Every attempt has been made by the Publisher to secure appropriate
permissions for material reproduced in this book. If there has been any
oversight we will be happy to rectify the situation in future editions or
reprints. Written submissions should be made to the Publisher.

British Library Cataloguing in Publication Data (CIP) is available
for this title.

Printed in Malta by Melita Press

ISBN 978 1 78322 142 4

Visit our website: www.readzonebooks.com

Pig in Love

by Vivian French
illustrated by Tim Archbold

READZONE

When Pig fell in love
With Piggie next door
He took her red roses –

Then took her some more.

"I love you, dear Piggie!
I hope you love me!

Why don't we get married?
Please say you agree!"

But Piggie said, "No!"
And started to cry.

"My daddy won't let me
Until pigs can fly!"

Our Pig was a hero.
He made himself wings

Of leather and feathers
And tied them with strings.

He marched to the hill
At the top of the town,

But he couldn't fly up –

He could only fly down.

Then Cow floated by
In her spotty balloon,

"Hey, you there –
Come with me!
I'm off to the moon!"

"Oh YES!" shouted Pig
And his Piggie together,

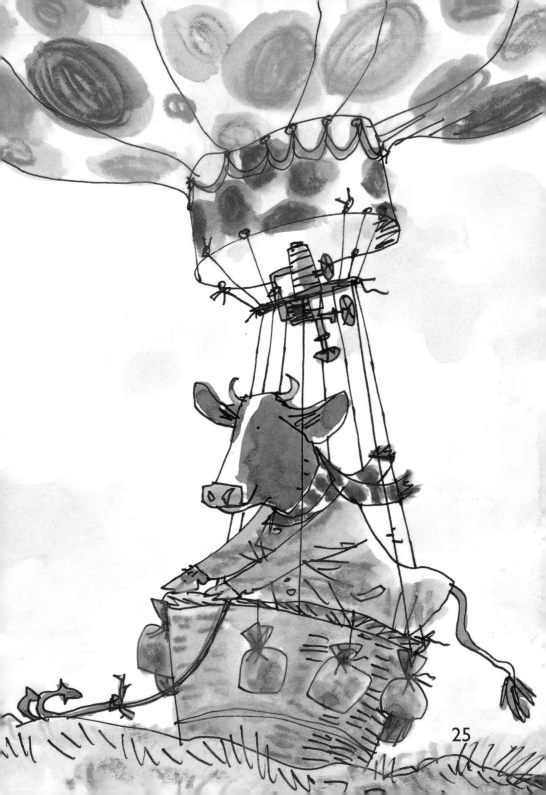

"Let's fly to the moon!

And we'll stay there for ever!"

So Pig and his Piggie
Flew off and away...

Were they happy? You bet!
And they're happy today.

Did you enjoy this book?

Look out for more *Redstarts* titles – first rhyming stories

Alien Tale by Christine Moorcroft and Cinza Battistel
ISBN 978 1 78322 135 6

A Mouse in the House by Vivian French and Tim Archbold
ISBN 978 1 78322 416 6

Batty Betty's Spells by Hilary Robinson and Belinda Worsley
ISBN 978 1 78322 136 3

Croc by the Rock by Hilary Robinson and Mike Gordon
ISBN 978 1 78322 143 1

Now, Now Brown Cow! by Christine Moorcroft and Tim Archbold
ISBN 978 1 78322 132 5

Old Joe Rowan by Christine Moorcroft and Elisabeth Eudes-Pascal
ISBN 978 1 78322 138 7

Pear Under the Stairs by Christine Moorcroft and Lisa Williams
ISBN 978 1 78322 137 0

Pie in the Sky by Christine Moorcroft and Fabiano Fiorin
ISBN 978 1 78322 134 9

Pig in Love by Vivian French and Tim Archbold
ISBN 978 1 78322 142 4

Tall Story by Christine Moorcroft and Neil Boyce
ISBN 978 1 78322 141 7

The Cat in the Coat by Vivian French and Alison Bartlett
ISBN 978 1 78322 140 0

Tuva by Nick Gowar and Tone Erikson
ISBN 978 1 78322 139 4